by Brenda Baker
illustrated by Maia Batumashvili

home sweet home

My Handsome husband, thank you for your loving support, encouragement and patience.
This one was a biggie. Moosey, it's official. You can now tell the world. Guanaleeta, you are my go-to guru
and I couldn't have done it without you! I sure love you guys.
-Brenda Baker

For my sons, Luka Beqa and Sandro. May they grow up happy and experience great success!
They are my hope and future.
-Maia Batumashvili

For information regarding perimssion, contact HeyDayPublishing @ www.heydaypublishing.com

ISBN-13: 978-1-7322868-3-2
ISBN-10: 1-7322868-3-3

Library of Congress Control Number: 2019912295

THE EATING OF TURKEYS
A POEM
BY GUSTAVO THE GOAT

I KNOW A SECRET
OF THANKSGIVING DAY
A TERRIBLE THING
WHERE THEY TAKE YOU AWAY!
AND EAT YOU!
IF YOU'RE A TURKEY.
BECAUSE YOU'RE TASTY.

AS A CONNOISSEUR OF KNOWLEDGE
IT'S MY MISSION TO SAY
TO **EVERY** TURKEY
COME THANKSGIVING DAY
THEY WILL FIND YOU.
AND EAT YOU!
BECAUSE YOU'RE TASTY.

THE END
HAPPY THANKSGIVING

'Twas the eve before T-Day
The feast menu was set,
And Tendra the turkey
Was feeling the threat
Of yams with marshmallows
And dried ears of corn.

Poor Tendra the turkey
Was feeling forlorn!

For she'd heard of
Past poultry
And the terrible feat
That all poultry persuasion
Eventually meet.

"On the day in November
Comes a day to remember…"

Gustavo began with a sigh.

"You'll be sitting and resting,
Perhaps even nesting,
Then suddenly, to your surprise!
They'll reach out and grab you
And straight up kidnap you
And dine on your succulent thighs.

And they'll eat you…

Because you're tasty."

"Is it true that they'll cook me?"
Wailed the poor,
Distressed foul.

"Then they'll wish on my wishbone?!"

She gasped with a scowl.

"This cannot be true!
I'm not that kind of bird,
I can speak Greek and Chinese!
I can even crochet,
I know how to buck hay
And make Graskaas,
A Dutch kind of cheese!"

Now, Tendra the turkey
Was naturally sweet.
(No, not the tasty
Sweet white meat you eat.)
She was kind, nice and wise
With big soulful eyes
(And apparently mouthwatering,
Delicious thighs)
And Tendra did NOT want to be someone's meal!

So Gustavo and Tendra made each other
A deal.

They came up with a plan
To hide her in plain sight.
They would start right away,
It was already night!
She would hide in disguise
'Til this whole thing blows over
Making Farmers revert
To next day leftovers.

A plan set in motion,
A most brilliant guise!
To devise an escape
And escape her demise.

Poor Tendra was nervous
And rightfully so!
For as the sun set
And the moon rose aglow,
She feared in her heart
That tomorrow would yield
A far less appealing frolic
In the grass field.

But Gustavo the goat,
Who was wily and clever,
Had a plan that was just as sneaky as ever!

"Now, don't you fret,
My tasty best friend.
We'll stop this whole thing
Put it all to an end.
The eating of turkeys
On Thanksgiving Day?
Who'd do such a thing?
Quite disgusting, I'd say."

So Gustavo and Tendra
Huddled 'round in the coop,
And they thought up ideas
To fool and to dupe
Those meat-eating Farmers
To make them forget
About succulent Tendra
And her tasty croquettes.

"We'll insert you here," Gustavo said with a shove.
"This haybale fits you,
Snug as a glove!"

But alas…

Though she slipped in with haybale
With ease,
Her legs were so long
You could still see her knees!

"Aaaahhh…aaahhhh…aaachhhooo!"

Not to mention Tendra has…

Allergies.

"I'm nervous of heights,"
Tendra chattered her beak.
"This ladder's too tall!" she began to shriek.

"Just go, rung by rung,
You'll get to the top!" Gustavo cheered on
As she started to stop.

"I can't do it, I'm scared!" Tendra nervously cried.

Gustavo's eyes widened
At the disturbing sight.
Tendra slipping and sliding
Her toenails gliding
Her confidence in herself
Quickly subsiding.
And then!
One by one,
And then!
Rung by rung,
Tendra completely fell down the ladder,
Landing upon her best goat friend's
Full bladder.

"Nothing is working,"
Tendra cried in distress.
"I'm no good at hiding
This whole thing's a mess!"

Gustavo grabbed hold
And he shook his foul friend.

"Now don't even fret,
This will not be the end!
I know of a place
So dark and so deep
That not one single Farmer
Would dare even creep."

And with that he plunged Tendra
Down deep in the feed.

"Just hold all your breath,
Or you'll choke on the seeds."

Tendra held her breath in
As Gustavo instructed,
But a quick little hiccup
Left her airway obstructed.

"I'm choking," Tendra quipped
As she started to cough.
"I can't take it, I need out!"

She'd had quite enough.

So Gustavo reached in
And pulled her up and out,
As a sprinkling of seeds
Fell out from her mouth.

"It's over, I'm doomed,"
Tendra started to sob.
"The sunshine is rising,
It's already dawn."

Tendra solemnly patted Gustavo's small head.
"Thank you, Gustavo, you've been a good friend."

But he would have none
Of what Tendra was saying!
"Now you stop all that nonsense,
This is just the beginning!
We'll just keep on looking,
There must be a place
To hide you and keep you
And make sure you're safe."

"I think it's too late," Tendra said quietly.

"WHAT EVER IS WRONG WITH SOCIETY?!"

Gustavo was now more determined
Than ever!
He must save her behind!
And be even more clever!
So Gustavo dug deep
In his genius brain
And he looked and he looked
'Til his eyes had eyestrain,
And his thoughts had all fused into one jumbled mess.
But then the suddenly

BAM!

His brain had a success.

"Look, Tendra, look!"
Gustavo yelled out.
"I've found it! It's perfect!
A perfect hideout!"

Tendra turned 'round
And she saw it, too!

A wheelbarrow,
On its side…
Painted light baby blue.

"We'll stick you right here
It's just the right fit!"

Tendra the turkey shimmied a bit,

And ducked in her head
And sucked in her feet
And then, just like that

Her disguise was complete.

"Now, don't make a peep," Gustavo whispered.

He'd done it!
He saved her!
He'd hidden the bird!

Gustavo danced 'round
With his happy, goat dance
Celebrating victory
Of this strange circumstance.

But then!

Just like that,
The barn door creaked open.
And wouldn't you know it?

Two Farmers stepped forward.

"Gobble gobble!" laughed one Farmer.

"Turkey time!" laughed the other.

And they ambled inside
High-fiving each other.

They looked high
And looked low
But no turkey was there.

They called and they called
But no turkey, nowhere.

"Hey, what's going on?" they both said, confused.

Gustavo watched on
Feeling giddy, amused.

*'They'll never find her,
She's hidden alright!
But they'll never find her
Hidden right in plain sight!'*

One Farmer took notice
At the goat's happy dance
And made an assumption
Of this current happenstance.

"I think he knows something," one said boorishly.
"Where is the turkey?
Tell us now,
Where is she?"

The Farmers closed right in on nervous Gustavo
Detecting a fault in the old goat's bravado.

"We know that she's in here,"
They began to yell.
"Where is the turkey?!"

But Gustavo rebelled.

He'd never tell them!
No, he'd never crack!
For both he and Tendra
Made a sacred pact.
Gustavo stood still
With no plans to spill beans
As Tendra watched on
Guiltily quarantined.

"Our plans have been ruined!"
The Farmers yelled on.
"Now that there's no turkey,
Thanksgiving's all gone..."

But then!

One Farmer grabbed Gustavo
And said,

"If we don't have a turkey,
I guess you'll do instead..."

Tendra erupted from her hiding place
And she raced quickly forward
At her most quickest pace!

"Wait, here I am!" she squawked
And she squealed.

"No!" Gustavo gasped,
"That's not part of the deal!
You should stay hidden,
I'll take the fall,
Get right back in there
You sneaky butterball!"

"I'll do no such thing!"
Tendra stubbornly stated.
"You're my very best friend
That fact can't be debated.
But you're my escape goat!
Not scapegoat, you see.
You will not take my place,
It's feasting day for me."

Tendra now visible
And completely in view
Of two ecstatic Farmers
Who knew what to do,

Gustavo could see in her eyes that she knew
As Tendra whispered softly,

"I'll miss you...adieu."

Without even a word
Without further delay
They each grabbed a wing

And led Tendra away.

Time stood eerily still
In that barn for that goat.

Gustavo sat speechless
A lump in his throat.

"Oh Tendra..." he whimpered.
"Why must this be your fate?
How could they just waltz in here
And confiscate
My very best friend..."

He sunk to the floor,
Filled with sad hopelessness.

But just as Gustavo
Laid down in distress,
Tendra BURST through the barn doors
In a brand-new headdress!
Made of corn cobs
And flowers
And marshmallows, too!
It had yams and cranberries
And dangly cashews!

She was fetchingly dressed
For some grand celebration,
Holding tight in her wing
A goat-sized invitation!

"TENDRA YOU'RE ALIVE!"

Gustavo screamed in delight.
"I can't believe it! You're here!"

"Here I am friend, surprise!"

Tendra sashayed to-and-fro for a bit,
"Do you like it? Does it suit me?
Do you like my outfit?"

Gustavo's jaw dropped.
He couldn't believe it!
Tendra. Alive! He ran to her quick.
Embracing her tightly
He asked her, "How?
How did you not end up as Farmer chow?
Did you ninja chop them
Into tiny Farmer bits?
Or did you sneak away quick
And escape those nitwits?"

"It turns out they're not nitwits,"
Tendra sang, gleefully.
"They're sophisticates,
And chose to invite ME!
I am THE guest of honor
This Thanksgiving Day.
So they gave me this crown
And goat-sized invitation
To invite you, Gustavo,
To our Thanksgiving celebration!"

Gustavo read the small note,
His heart full with delight,
For he too was invited
On this very night
To dine with the Farmers
And his bestest friend
And eat snacks and tell stories
Until the day's end.

A full veggie feast
Was on the menu
With radishes, pies
And asparagus stew.
And pineapples, marshmallows
And bok choy barbeque.

They danced all around
What a happy occasion!
Thanksgiving for all,
What a grand celebration!

With Tendra in her headdress
And Gustavo in tow,
Both sashayed their ways
To the farmhouse below,
Where a glorious feast
Was waiting for them
And they both said goodbye
To the day's start mayhem.

Now Farmers and turkeys
And goats and the like
Would all dine on dinner
And sing through the night.

"Happy Thanksgiving!
We're so glad you're here!
Let's raise up a glass
And toast to good cheer!
We're glad that we're healthy!
We're glad for fall, too!
We're glad for these snacks,
And we're glad we have you!"

The Celebrating of Turkeys
A Poem
By the Farmers

Thanksgiving is time
For time honored traditions
And also creating some new definitions.
So on this special day
We're honoring you!
Tendra the turkey
We salute you!
We're glad you're with us
We say this gratefully,
That all here are welcome
Under earth's canopy
Because, to us,
We're all one family.

Happy Thanksgiving!